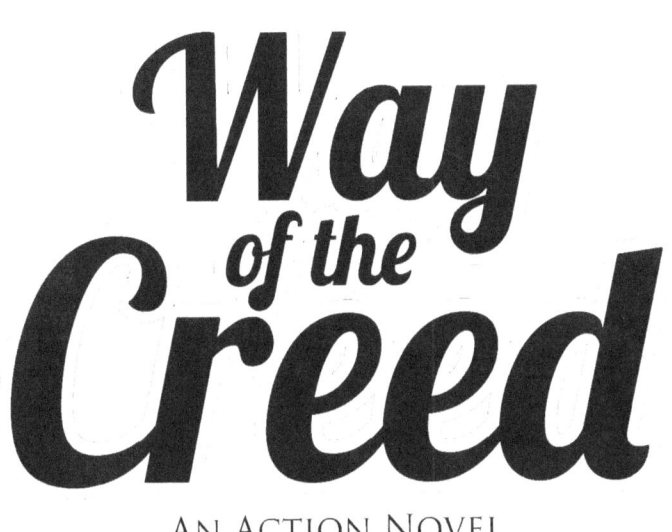

Way of the Creed

AN ACTION NOVEL

ORMENA UKPU

ISBN: 978-1-945532-15-3

Published, edited and illustrated by:
Opportune Independent Publishing Company

Printed in the United States of America

For permission requests, write to the publisher, addressed
"Attention: Permissions Coordinator," at the address below.

info@opportunepublishing.com
www.opportunepublishing.com

To purchase this book in bulk, or for special orders, visit:
www.wayofthecreed.com.

DEDICATION

For Mom and Dad, with gratitude and love.

ACKNOWLEDGMENTS

There are many people who helped bring this book to life, but seven individuals deserve special thanks:

Roman Searfini, my third grade friend at McNeil Elementary, who was interested in how I was developing the story, and also instrumental in helping me to incorporate the shark pet idea.

Luis Vasquez, another third grade friend at McNeil Elementary, who drew the first sketches I used as samples, and to inspired the illustration of the book's characters.

Mael Cisneros, my friend at McNeil Elementary's YMCA after school program, who played the editor's role while I was drafting the story. He wasn't afraid to push my imagination.

Mrs. Elizabeth DeRouen and **Mrs. Kim Leonard**, my third grade teachers who let me do autonomous writing in class with my buddies, when we have spare time.

My Dad and Mom, **Bernard** and **Maureen**, without whose incredible support, this book would not have become a reality.

SYNOPSIS

Mason Wills has been in jail for seven years. He was first brought to jail after his attack on President John Frederick. Although this makes him seem like a bad guy, he actually did it because President Frederick was not governing the town of Creedwoods fairly. The town had become so corrupt, that if you didn't work for President Frederick without pay, he would kill you. But he wasn't alone; his team of soldiers, better known as the President Federal Team (PFT), backed him up every time. Unlike the other towns' people, this team was paid for their work. So, Mason, the captain of The Creed, gathered his team in order to end the unfair practice and to bring peace to Creedwoods at last.

CHAPTER ONE

MASON'S ESCAPE

MASON HAS BEEN IN JAIL for nearly seven years for his attack on President John Frederick. It hasn't been an easy time; sometimes he would get mad and punch other prisoners. But one day he escaped. How, you ask? Well, first, two prisoners were fighting because one didn't like how the other looked at him. So everyone in the prison started to get mad and one by one, they started fighting.

Soon the guards came. Mason knew in order to make his plan work, he had to fight the guards while everyone else was fighting. As he punched and kicked, he successfully stole the keys from the belt of one of the guards. Soon after, he was in his Mustang GT 300, driving away from the prison.

Mason drove to a spot where he'd left his boat that he has had since he was 9 years old. But to his surprise, he found crooks on his boat, walking around looking for things. He took out his sword and sliced each of their ears off. Then he took the cell phone from one of the crooks' pocket to call his crew. All he said was, "I'm out of that stupid prison." "Alright, we are on our way." said his friend, Renov. "No, no, no - if I go back to the base, I bet you when they find out I'm gone, they're going to go straight there to find me!"

MASON WILLS HAS BEEN IN JAIL FOR SEVEN YEARS.

said Mason. "Yeah, you got a point," said Renov. "Renov, meet me and the crew at Kentucky," said Mason.

Four hours later, Mason was reunited with his crew. Before they could even high-five, Renov shouted, "Oh shoot - I see them, duck!" As the President Federal Team (PFT) fired their shotguns, Mason, Renov, Ryan, Woods and Bowman took out their rifles and fired back. When Mason and his crew took out the PFT soldiers, one of their captains came out of nowhere. "Uh oh," said Renov. This PFT captain did not look like the rest of the soldiers.

The captain took out his bloody sword from his pocket. Then Mason took out his sword and they began to fight. After a few seconds, Mason said, "You have no chance of beating me." "Are you sure about that?" the Captain asked. "Yeah I'm sure," said Mason. Then the PFT captain tripped Mason with his sharp sword. As soon as he tripped Mason, he was about to stab him, but Renov shot the Captain in the head before he had the chance.

Mason pushed the body of the captin off himself. "Thanks for saving my life, Renov," said Mason. "You're welcome Mason," said Renov. "Now what do we do?" asked Renov.

"We bring the PFT WAR!" said Mason.

As they walked to the boat, Mason announced, "We are going to Minnesota today boys!" All of the crew cheered , "yay!" Then Bowman said, "I think I see a PFT boat." "There it is, you can see the logo!" said Mason. They quickly used their canons to sink the boat. The PFT also tried to sink Mason's crews' boat, but failed. As the boat slowly sunk into the deep blue water in the middle of the ocean, the entire crew cheered together.

Although they were victorious, Mason did not seem ok. So Renov asked him was he alright. "No, somethings fishy." Mason replied. As the words were coming out of his mouth, out jumped two megalodons. "I thought they were extinct!" Shouted Renov. "They are not here to kill us. They are here to kill the PFT," said Woods. "They are my pets, Victor and Striker," said Mason. "Victor and Striker?" asked Renov.

CHAPTER TWO

THE TRAIN OF THE MEGALODONS

THESE WERE, IN FACT, HIS PETS, and it was time to train them. So Mason cracked his knuckles to prepare.

"Ryan why are you so quiet?" Asked Woods. "Because I don't have much to do." Said Ryan. "Yes you do, you can drive the boats, cars and planes," said Mason. Ryan looked, but did not respond. Ever since that day, Mason knew something was up with that kid. "Victor, do you see that boat?" asked Mason. "I want you to go break it down!" Victor roared very loudly.

"Striker, you're going to go ahead and attack that great white shark right there, to the right of the boat. Striker roared so loudly that Mason went deaf for eight straight seconds. When Striker smelled something bloody, he hit the boat Mason was on. Mason jumped out and said, "Whoa!" Mason knew something wasn't right. When Mason got back on the boat, Ryan tried to attack him with a knife. Luckily, Mason blocked it. "What are you doing?" asked Mason. "Killing you!" yelled Ryan. "The only reason I joined your side was to get information!" said Ryan. "What?!" yelled Mason, in confusion. "You're a TRAITOR!" said Mason. Mason quickly took out his sword in an attempt to kill him, but Renov ran over and blocked him. "We need him for information about the PFT," said Renov. Mason agreed and tied Ryan up with the ropes. While Mason left to get more rope, Renov guarded him to make sure he wouldn't escape. Before Mason returned, Ryan was able to free one hand in order to punch

Renov in the face.

With only a few seconds to get away, he jumped overboard and tried to swim his way back to the PFT, but he couldn't swim that far. He found a piece of floating bark to grab ahold to and float. The strong waves eventually took him back to shore of the PFT base. The PFT were surprised to see old Ryan back at the base. Ryan spoke French to his partners. "Bonjour les partenaries, je avoir venu arrière avec informations de le Creed." said Ryan. Translation: Hello partners, I have come back with information from The Creed. He was filled with so much pride that he wasn't ready for the news to come. "Our captain is DEAD," said his partner. "What, how, by who!?" asked Ryan. "By that evil assassin, Bryce Green," whispered his partner. "Anthony, we will bring war to The Creed and to Bryce!" screamed Ryan. "Oh, and since Captain Frank is dead, we did a vote between you and I to be captain and you won," said Anthony. "Oh my gosh, it's a dream come true!" said Ryan, with great joy. "Now we bring the Creed and Green WAR!" said Ryan. All the PFT cheered.

WITH ONLY A FEW SECONDS TO GET AWAY, HE JUMPED OVERBOARD AND TRIED TO SWIM HIS WAY BACK TO THE PFT, BUT HE COULDN'T SWIM THAT FAR.

CHAPTER THREE

A NEW MAN?

BACK AT MASON'S BASE there was a knock on the door. When Renov opened the door, there was a man with a sword standing there waiting. "How can I help you?" said Renov. The man swiftly put his sharp sword up against Renov's neck. The man had a nametag that read: "Bryce Green." "Have you seen the PFT?" asked the man. Mason hurried to pick up his pistol to point at the man. Then the man grabbed Renov, straining his neck. "Put the pistol down, or your friend dies," said the man. Bowman said, "Wait! Did you say you were looking for the PFT?" "Yeah, do you work for them?" said the man. "No, we were trying to destroy them," said Renov. After realizing they had a common enemy, Mason asked the man, "Now can you let go of my friend?" "Oh yeah, sure," said the man.

"Would you like to join our team?" asked Mason. "Um join, first of all, you guys are a tiny group, second of all, your base is lame," said the man. "Ok I can agree with the tiny group one, but not the lame part." If you want to see this base go wild, we can get out of the normal mode quickly.

"Woods, hit the button!" demanded Mason with a smirk on his face. After just a few seconds, the base had changed entirely into a massive fort; there were so many guns, planes, boats, and even awesome cars. The man was amazed and couldn't believe all the powerful machinery he saw in front of him. "Yeah, ok I'm joining the team," said the man. He then properly introduced himself, "Name's Bryce Green." "Mason Wills," said Mason.

"Where's your original team?" asked Mason. "Oh I got thousands of them, they are at my base," said Bryce. "So I'll be right back so I can get my team and my base connected to yours," said Bryce. "Okay dozy," said Mason.

Four hours later... "I'm back," yelled Bryce. "We will have all the people helping us to defeat the PFT," said Bryce.

WE BRING THE
PFT WAR!

CHAPTER FOUR

THE
GREAT WHITE EATS

"HAVE I TOLD YOU ABOUT OUR SHARK PETS?" Mason asked. "What pets?" Asked Bryce. "Okay, then I haven't told you," said Mason. "So one day in the Atlantic ocean my crew and I were just enjoying the cruise." "Lol the rhymes," laughed Bryce. "Shhh, I'm telling the story," said Mason. "Then while I was getting my life jacket, two megalodons jumped up out of nowhere. They landed on our boat, which was too much weight for it. So the boat started to quickly sink. Everyone ended up in the water with the two humongous beasts. Both started coming after me, so I swam as fast and hard as I could. Before I knew it, the two megalodons caught up to me, so I closed my eyes in fear of what was next to come.

All of a sudden, I started to feel licking on me. All of us were surprised at what happened. After that, Bowman said 'what did you eat?' I replied, 'meat and steak'. 'No wonder,' said Bowman. 'Maybe the sharks like you because of the meat and steak you ate.' You're right, I said. So then the sharks used their tails to throw me on their backs. They did the same with the others. So that's how I got my pet sharks," said Mason. "Hmm can I get a pet shark?" asked Bryce, sounding and looking jealous. "I don't know, maybe you need to

BOTH STARTED COMING AFTER ME, SO I SWAM AS FAST AND HARD AS I COULD.

eat meat or steak," said Mason. "Okay whatever you say," said Bryce.

So Bryce decided to eat a whole lot of steak. He got so full that his stomach was growling. Then he rode his horse to the ocean shore to get on Mason's boat. Mason and everyone else were following from behind. They made it to the ocean, but no sharks were spotted. Bryce got so frustrated and started shooting in the ocean to drive some attention. Then a fin that looked like a shark came. It jumped up and went for Bryce. It was a great white shark. Then it opened its mouth and tried to bite Bryce. The shark got Bryce in its mouth and swallowed Bryce firmly in. Mason and everyone was flabbergasted at what had just happened. Before everyone could even think of a plan, they jumped in the boat to head home to devise a new plan. Now, with Bryce gone, how can they still defeat the PFT?

To be continued....

ABOUT THE AUTHOR

Ormena Ukpu autonomously started writing stories in second grade at McNeil Elementary School. In third grade, at 9 years old, he started a book club called Robooks. He got 13 pupils to join the club to write books. They wrote several incoherent manuscripts with title such as "Prison Life", "Jet Wars," and "New Football Legends".

After the Spring break in 2016, one day, Ormena came from school looking sad. He told his father that he's unhappy because everyone in his book club quit. He said they were no longer interested in writing since they were not being paid. His father encouraged him to keep writing. While he was working on Way of the Creed, behold three of his friends at school got interested again in working with him shortly before their break for the summer. He finished Way of the Creed in the summer of 2016.

Currently, Ormena is a 4th grader at the Harmony Science Academy at Katy, Texas. He is working on the second series of Way of the Creed.

Ormena is available at www.wayofthecreed.com